The Wizard's Wish

Or, How He Made the Yuckies Go Away
- A Story About the Magic in You

Story and Pictures by

Brad Yates

For my family: thank you for your loving support and patience.

ISBN: 1451570902
ISBN-13: 9781451570908
Library of Congress Control Number: 2010905103

Many years ago, even before your parents were born, there was a peaceful village in a faraway land. The people who lived there were very happy, especially the children.

They would laugh and play, and even when they were in school or helping around the house, they were cheerful and felt good about themselves and what they were doing.

Oh, they felt other feelings, too, sometimes. That's a normal part of life. Sometimes they were afraid, sometimes angry, sometimes worried, sometimes sad. But they would talk to a friend, or get a hug, and the uncomfortable feelings rarely lasted very long.

When anyone felt really out of sorts, he would visit the wise and friendly wizard who lived with his pet owl in a small house just outside of the village.

With some magical spells, a variety of potions, and a wave of his wand, the wizard would help the person quickly return to his natural happy and healthy self.

One day, a terrible storm blew through the land, with dark clouds, strong winds, thunder, lightning, and a downpour of rain.

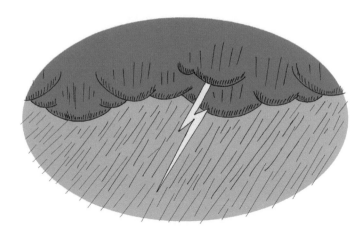

The people were very frightened. They ran for shelter, closed their doors and windows, and hid inside.

Fortunately, the storm quickly passed with little damage to the village.

But something was different.

Not long after the storm, the wizard noticed that more and more people were coming to see him. A lot of people were complaining of yucky feelings. And the wizard noticed that their yucky feelings were taking longer to go away.

When people got angry, they stayed angry longer. Some people felt sad or scared and didn't even know why.

They found it difficult to keep their minds on what they needed to do. They didn't even play sports as well as they used to.

Many of the children were throwing tantrums, and nearly every child was having trouble getting to sleep, because they were afraid of each little noise at night. And when they had a test at school, they were so tired or nervous and distracted that they could barely pass it (and sometimes they didn't).

The wizard soon found that each day he was working longer and longer, sometimes well into the night. He found he sometimes had to turn people away until the next day!

"What could be going on?" he wondered.

The problem seemed to be spreading. It was as if there was something in the air.

And there was.

And ... it wasn't long before the wizard caught it.

He found himself becoming very grouchy. He knew something must be wrong, as he was usually very cheerful. But now all these people expected him to help them, and he was feeling quite yucky himself.

He thought and thought and thought about this problem. And, as he often did while thinking, he gently tapped his wand against his head.

"Oh, how I wish I knew how to solve this. Think, think, think!" he said as he tap, tap, tapped.

Then, almost suddenly, he noticed that he was feeling better. He found this rather odd.

What was even odder was that something small seemed to have fallen out of his ear and onto his desk. Something quite small indeed! So small that a normal person could not see it, but wizards have particularly keen eyesight.

And magnifying glasses.

"What is this?" he wondered.

As he took a closer look, it appeared to be some sort of creature, and a nasty one at that. Since he was feeling better now, he knew what must have happened.

"Oho! So, you're the little bug that's been bothering me, eh?" the wizard said. "You've made me feel quite yucky. I suppose I will call you a Yucky." But then, right before his eyes, the yucky shriveled up and vanished! It could not survive once it had been tapped out.

The wizard was amazed and excited. Tapping on his head with his wand made the yucky go away! But how had this happened? He immediately went searching through his magical books for answers. The wizard loved to learn, and he had a wonderful library of books. He studied long into the night, looking for clues about the mysterious little creature that had been causing him to feel upset, and how it had gone away.

Because wizards can travel quickly by magic, he even traveled to the four corners of the world, searching for answers.

(This was before they knew the world was round.)

Finally, in an ancient scroll he found in China, he learned that the human body had magical energy that moved along little pathways, like tiny rivers.

He learned that when the flow was smooth, people felt good. When the flow was stopped, people felt bad.

Perhaps these little creatures blew in with that storm, the wizard thought. *They must somehow stop the healthy flow of energy and then people feel yucky.*

The scroll also showed a map of points along the energy pathways that were like little buttons that help make the magic flow better. He learned that it was one of these points he had tapped with his wand.

"Ah, now I see," said the wizard to his owl. "When I tap these points, the magic gets stronger and the yuckies are forced out. Now I know what to do to help my friends."

The next day, as people started coming to see him again, the wizard began tapping on different magic points according to the old map.

Sure enough, as he did so, the little creatures started popping out of people's ears.

As he tapped, the wizard talked about the yuckies, saying things like, "My, this is a bad case of grouchiness," or, "This certainly is a very sad feeling."

It seemed they liked to be talked about and would show up in people's ears to hear better. And as the wizard tapped the magic points, they were forced out, and they disappeared.

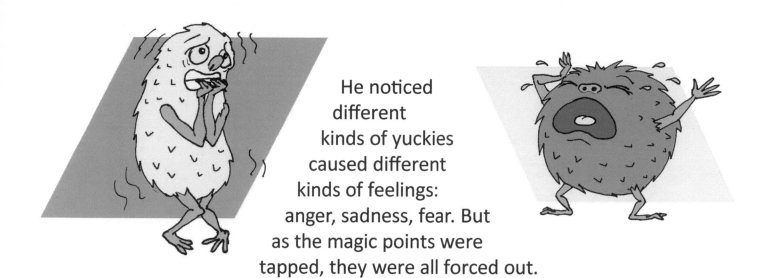

He noticed different kinds of yuckies caused different kinds of feelings: anger, sadness, fear. But as the magic points were tapped, they were all forced out.

The yuckies were all so small that the people couldn't really see them, but as the wizard tapped, they did notice they started to feel better.

Some people felt better very quickly, and some took a little longer. Some had more than one yucky that needed to be tapped out. But the tapping helped everyone. It was clear that no matter who the person was, young or old, rich or poor, they all had this magic inside of them.

But even though the wizard was helping people quickly, there were still many more people seeking help. As he watched people talking, he noticed that the bad feelings seemed almost contagious.

"The yuckies must be spreading!" the wizard cried.
"I'll never be able to help all these people!
There are so many, and I'm just one wizard!"

That night, he studied some more, and thought some more, looking for a solution.

"Sigh ... I wish the people could help me help them. If only they could help themselves," he said as he tapped his wand against his own forehead.

"If only ..." He stared at the magic map, and then it hit him.

"That's it!" he yelled so loudly he scared half the feathers off his owl. "The magic is already inside people! They can tap on themselves!"

He immediately set to work making copies of the magic points map.

The next day, as more and more people arrived at his home to be cured, he greeted them with great excitement.

"I have wonderful news!" he shouted. "You have the power to heal yourselves of the yuckies; you just need to tap into it! You can tap on yourselves!"

There was silence. The people didn't know quite how to respond.

Finally, someone said, "But … we're not magicians."

"The magic is already inside you!" the wizard answered with a knowing smile.

"We don't know where to tap," said another in the crowd.

"I've made maps for you!" replied the wizard with an even bigger smile.

"But we don't have wands!" several people said all at once.

"I … er, you … ummmm …" At this, the wizard's smile went away. He was stuck. He stood there staring at the crowd, not knowing what to say. And as he thought, he did what he often did: he tapped. But this time, he wasn't holding his wand. All he had to tap with was his finger.

And as he tapped, he noticed something. He could feel that the magic was working. He was feeling better, even without his wand!

"Aha! You *do* have wands!" the wizard insisted. "Your fingers will do the trick. The solution has been right here at our fingertips all along!"

The wizard began passing the maps out to the people and showing them how to tap. He even had them use two fingers, to make their "wands" double strong. But there was still some concern that, not being magicians, they could not make it work.

The wizard thought to himself, *Even though they aren't wizards, I know they can do this.* And then he had an idea.

"Silly me. Of course! You need magic words to set up the spell," he told them. "Repeat after me: Even though I am not a wizard, I can still do magic!"

He had them repeat these words three times while tapping on one of the magic points.

Then the wizard guided the villagers to tap along the other points on the map.

As they tapped, they talked about the yucky feelings they had and also how they wanted to feel.

Almost immediately, yuckies started popping out of people's ears, and smiles began returning to the faces of the villagers.

Some people felt silly doing the tapping. Some of them even seemed to prefer holding onto their yuckies rather than look foolish. But eventually, seeing that others were feeling better, and since almost everyone else was doing it, they said, "Even though I look silly, I guess I'll tap anyway." And they were glad they did.

As people were tapping, other spells were created, all beginning with the magic words, "Even though …"

Some said, "Even though I feel bad, I want to feel great!"

Others said, "Even though I have these problems, I'm still a nice person."

And a spell that seemed very powerful was, "Even though I feel yucky, I really love myself."

It seemed that when two or more people tapped together, they felt better faster. But even those who tapped by themselves felt relief.

Yuckies were being knocked out of people left and right, and they vanished in the sunlight.

As the people began feeling better, they went home and taught the tapping to their family and friends. Within a short while, the village was happier than it had ever been.

People were able to do what they needed to do, even better than they had before. They even played sports better.

The children were happy and playful and helpful again, and they were able to get to sleep easily.

They even did much better at school.

The villagers also noticed that they felt really good about themselves and were much kinder to themselves. And they noticed something else: the better they felt, the more good things happened to them. It was as if being happy made them lucky. Their lives were becoming more magical.

They also found that they were nicer to one another. When they felt good about themselves, it seemed impossible to be hurtful to anyone else.

And they understood that when someone else was being mean, it was because that person felt yucky.

Sometimes feelings that didn't feel so good still came up, which was normal. But these feelings didn't last long, and people were able to help themselves and others feel better much more quickly. People knew when they had yuckies, and they just tapped them away.

And when they felt they could use a little extra magic, they would go to see the wizard, who was happy to help.

To thank the wise wizard who had helped them unlock their personal magic, the villagers held a great celebration in his honor.

As the people toasted him, the wizard said, "You know, it's always possible that more yuckies might show up."

The people looked at each other and began smiling. Then, all together, they raised their "magic wands" in the air and said, "We'll be ready for them!"

And now, so will you.

A Wish Come True for Parents and Teachers
(and anyone else who loves children!)

Ever wished you had a simple and quick way to help your child (or yourself) feel better?

While yucky feelings might not really be caused by little creatures, the tapping process the wizard used in this book really does help people feel better. It is based on a real technique called Emotional Freedom Techniques, or EFT. This is a wonderful technique for removing the negative emotions that limit our happiness and success. Using this technique, you can gain the emotional freedom to truly pursue being, doing, and having what you really want in life.

EFT is a meridian-based energy therapy developed by Gary Craig from the landmark discoveries of Dr. Roger Callahan. This book is presented with deep gratitude to these two men. Based on the same principles as acupuncture, EFT is a simple technique that often provides rapid relief from physical-emotional issues (e.g. fear, anger, sadness, worry, cravings, nightmares, physical pain, and much more). It can also clear the negative thoughts that block our best performance, freeing us up to improve in any area of life, including academics and sports.

While EFT has yielded impressive results in treating physical and psychological issues, not everyone will benefit in the same way. Brad Yates is not a doctor, and the information presented here is not intended to replace appropriate treatment by a physician or mental health professional. The instructions on the following page can provide great benefit in feeling better, but are only a brief introduction to EFT. There have been no documented negative side effects from using EFT, and there should be no problem with your child doing the tapping as described here. However, different people require different care, and you must take responsibility for your child's well-being as well as your own. If you have any concerns, please consult a doctor prior to using this technique.

For more information about EFT, fun activities for kids, tapping videos, and other great resources, please visit: www.thewizardswish.com

How To Tap Away Yuckies

Decide what the yucky feeling is that you want to tap out and give it a name, such as: fear, pain, anger at someone, etc. Then, gently tapping with your "magic wand" (index and middle finger) on the side of your other hand, repeat this statement three times:

"Even though I have this _____ (yucky feeling, fear, pain, anger, etc.), I'm a really great kid." (Or, "I really love myself," or similar positive words.)

Then tap on each of the following energy points (shown in the picture) while talking about the yucky feeling:

1. Top of Head
2. Eyebrow
3. Side of Eye
4. Under Eye
5. Under Nose
6. Chin
7. Collarbone
8. Under Arm

Then take a deep breath.

You can even just say the same thing (yucky feeling, fear, etc.) on each point, or talk about how you want to feel (great, happy, etc.). Tap each point about seven times (that's a good magic number). You can tap with either hand on either side of the face and body. You can tap through the points once, or keep tapping a couple of rounds to help yourself feel better and better.

About the Author

Brad Yates is co-author of the best-seller *Freedom at Your Fingertips* and a featured expert in the film *The Tapping Solution*. He is also a graduate of Ringling Bros. & Barnum & Bailey Clown College, and has performed children's theatre around the world. Brad spends much of his time tapping with people to help them live their best life possible. Sometimes he does this by phone, sometimes in live workshops, and sometimes in videos on YouTube. And sometimes he's learning to play the guitar (or other fun stuff). He lives in Northern California with his wonderful wife and their two magnificent children.

www.thewizardswish.com

Made in the USA
Lexington, KY
11 October 2014